Ides of May

Devil's Land Stories

Terry Hooker

Published by Blue Dahlia Publishing House, 2023.

IDES OF MAY

First edition. March 21, 2023.

Copyright © 2023 Terry Hooker.

ISBN: 979-8215151389

Written by Terry Hooker.

Table of Contents

Authors Note | Cimarron County Oklahoma is the westernmost county in Oklahoma. Throughout most of history Cimarron has had the smallest population in Oklahoma. Cimarron is known to have the lowest precipitation rate yet the highest snowfall rate. | In the past the area had been known as no mans land and was the place where many outlaws went seeking refuge. | During the depression and the dust bowl Cimarron County was one of the most effected areas in the country, with drought, tornadoes, blizzards, floods and dirt storms the people of the area had to do whatever they could to survive, this included selling their children. | The characters in this book are fiction, but the hard times are based on real events. 47

To my amazing husband, look honey I didn't kill you in this one!

Chapter one
I am a Baby

In the grand scheme of the universe, I am a baby. Well, at least in this vessel I am. I, as an entity, have been around from the beginning of time itself. Within the realm I come from, I am King! I have been King for millennia there. I dwell in the nether along with those that existed before me, as well as those that came after. I can't tell you how we came to be. We just were and are. We fought, we thrived, and a few of us became beyond powerful while the rest lived to serve. The only downside to any of this, the nether, the power, and the existence, is that we cannot go where we pleased on the upside. We were trapped in the nether world with no chance ourselves to be free in the above. We had to wait to be called by those who thought they could control us.

HA!

Little did they know how powerful one must be to have even just an inkling of control over us. For we are the power they use to call us, the hate they thrive on, and those who shall live forever.

This vessel is still young and beautiful. Even though in human years, she would be considered ancient, well, that might be an exaggeration, some of your grandparents might be her age, but since you refer to them as ancient, that's how I refer to myself, well ourself. It might be a bit overwhelming once you realize there are two of us in here. But listen to our story, and you will come to understand.

I came into existence in this form in the modern year of 1935. It was in the middle of what was being called the Great Depression and the Dust Bowl. These were great times for my kind. We thrived on the suffering of mankind. There was no food or work. Money wasn't just tight, it was nonexistent. We trolled the netherworld waiting for some unsuspecting soul to summon us, to ask our assistance to make their lives better. But I digress; let's have the girl tell the story of the before.

You see, we share space, her and I. We. When we are working together, we are...well, We. Otherwise, she is her, and I am me. Do you understand? Good, I am so glad. Okay love, step up, and tell your story. That's it, good girl. Our voice will become quieter, and our thoughts will become calmer. She always has a way of bringing calm to our storm.

Chapter Two
The Family

We was, I mean were, he doesn't like when I don't talk correctly, we were farmers, or trying to be farmers I should say, in Cimarron County, Oklahoma when it happened. My father had passed away from excessive drinking. He liked the hooch. He liked the hooch more than he liked most anything else. I was not sorry to see him go. He was not a good man, but since we are being honest right now, mamma was not a good woman either, and she was who I was left with.

I will never forget that day. It started on a typical day; I was sixteen years old at the time. Nothing particularly special about me except I had been told I had an hourglass figure. Many people called me voluptuous. I just thought it was annoying. People stared, boys mostly, but girls did too. The girls whispered loud enough to hear them. "Whore." Honestly, I didn't even know what that word meant. I had heard people say it about my mamma, so I thought it just meant a mean, nasty person. Of course, I knew I wasn't mean or nasty, but since mamma was in loads, both mean and nasty, maybe they thought I was too.

I was average height with dishwater-colored eyes and mousy brown hair that hadn't been washed in way too long. My dress was made from leftover cloth scraps from when my mamma had made her own wardrobe. She always did her best to look above her station, even in what should have been her grief after daddy passed. She had to have as close to fancy clothes as she could make. She knew she couldn't just pass on clothes to me; I was not the same shape as her. I had to have things made or bought, but nothing was purchased new anymore. No, we were lucky to have anything at all, let alone new. She never made me anything, but she would pass the dresses that she didn't think were in style to me. She would cut them up first, so even if I had wanted to try to put one on, I couldn't, nope. She didn't want me to wear anything similar to what she did. So I would take the cut up dresses and piece together something for me to wear when I could.

There were four of us kids, we had to share the leftover cloth and hope it was enough to cover us. It was always easier for me to make my little brother and sister clothes. I could make smaller things for them; honestly, they didn't care much about what they looked like as long as they could go out and play. For me, it was harder to make clothes. My breasts were so big it never felt like there was enough fabric to cover them. It was always stretched tight over my chest. The buttons always gaped so you could see right in my shirt. I did my best to wear under clothes, but sometimes I didn't have any, or one of the littles needed them more than me.

Mama said it was indecent, yet she never held any fabric aside to make sure I was modestly covered. I constantly pulled and tugged at my clothes, trying to stay covered as I marched around the farmyard doing my chores. We had lost all our crops, and our hog had been killed by wild dogs. All we had left was a garden and chickens. I tried my best to make eggs in as many different ways as possible, but without anything else in the pantry, we often fell back to scrambled eggs with whatever vegetables I could salvage. It was a wonder I wasn't just skin and bones, The way my mamma went on and ate as much as she wanted, leaving us to split the rest. I always made sure that the littles had enough food, then tried to eat what was left, if there was anything. I would try to eat things directly out of the garden since this was the only time I didn't have to share with anyone, and sometimes we would catch a big fat rat or a squirrel. If we were really lucky, we would find a rabbit. But mostly, it was just eggs and vegetables for us all to split.

I wasn't the oldest, my brother, Peter, was. He took after our father, which meant that he was wholly unreliable. He made sure his hair was greased just right, his clothes looked good as could be, and he always had some smokes. I wasn't sure where he got the money for them, but I wasn't about to ask. He would have smacked me halfway across the house if I had questioned him. Then he would have laughed about it as he lit a smoke and left. On the other hand, maybe I should have asked him more, then he would've left us alone and not come 'round much.

Peter never took care of anything around the house. He just got in the way, ate, and got things dirty. It was up to me to tend to the little ones and make sure there was food on the table. I'd spend all day watching the babies and the animals and cleaning up. It was how life was; there was no way out that I could figure. I was just gonna spend my days cleaning up after people forever, either here or someplace else. I had no education, no money, and mamma said I had no looks. I was stuck in this ungodly life until the man showed.

Chapter Three

Fate

He wasn't the oldest man I had ever seen, but he was still pretty old. He had a grizzled beard that hung down to the middle of his chest. His grey hair was long and hung twisted and frazzled down his back. He wore all grey. His clothes weren't new, but they weren't old either. They seem to have been well taken care of. Even though his hair and beard were all over the place, he seemed as though he were clean and presented himself well. If I could put my finger on it, I would say at one time, he had money.

When I think back on him now, everything about him was grey. His hair, his beard, his clothes. He seemed to exude this grey cloud around himself. Almost as if he didn't want anyone to notice anything extraordinary about him. Yet, he exuded a type of power. It was palpable. You could feel it pushing against you as he moved closer. Of course, after what was to occur, maybe I am just projecting, but I swear he had power even then.

He opened our little front gate like he owned the place. No hesitation, no looking around. He just flipped the latch, opened it, walked through, then closed it back behind him again. All in one smooth motion. I saw him open it from where I stood on the back porch. I could see up and down the road a bit from there, too. There was nothing to show how he had gotten out to us. No car or horse. No wagon or any cloud of dust to show where he had been dropped off by someone else. We weren't too far out of town as a crow flies, but we were quite the walk. I know. I had to make that walk into town about once a week to see if there was anything we could sell or beg from people. The man wasn't out of breath like I usually was after that walk, nor was he sweaty in any way. I was sure that after going to town, I was sweaty and smelled of cut onions from not bathing. But here he was, looking as if he had just appeared at our gate.

He sauntered up to the front door and knocked.

Mamma opened the door as if she were opening the door to a mansion, not our crappy little clapboard house. She smiled in what I assume she thought was an alluring way. She leaned seductively on the door frame; I could hear her ask the man in a fake southern accent what brought him to her home. I didn't hear the answer but heard her bellowing for me not a second later.

"Annick, Annick! Where are you! Come inside. There is someone here who'd like to meet you."

I stopped where I was, the scraps for the chickens hanging in the bucket at my side. I remember looking at our few hens and contemplating whether I should pretend I didn't hear her, continue moving ahead so my chores would not get behind, and we would have dinner on the table that evening. I took in the dirty little yard, the broken down barn, my own tattered clothes and thought nothing could be worse than this, maybe just maybe, this man came to take me away to start a new life.

Maybe just maybe, I could be more than Annick, who wears old clothes and cooks scraps for dinner. I made my decision and placed the pail on the ground, and headed toward the house. I straightened my hair as best I could before tentatively walking into the house.

"Oh, there you are, my dear, don't be shy. Come all the way in the room and meet Mr. Smith." Her smile was faker than I had ever seen as she pushed me into the room in front of the grizzled man.

"Turn around. Let him look at you." She motioned for me to do a small turn. "As you see, she has some wonderful assets. Once she gets cleaned up a bit, I think you would be very, very happy with her."

I stood gaping at my mother as she spoke. As horrible as she was, I never in my whole life thought she would try to sell me. Somehow I thought that being my mother, she wouldn't think of me as something that she could use to earn a little money. My heart was in my throat as I realized to her I was just another thing to be used. From the corner of my eye, I could see my little brother and sister peeking in through the back door, trying to stay out of sight, but I could always see where they were. That was my job. To make sure they were safe. If she sold me to this man, who would keep them safe? I scowled in their direction and heard them scurry off.

The man approached me but did not touch me even when my mother encouraged him. "You see how nice and rounded her bottom is and how heavy her breasts are? She would make you a wonderful companion."

"Yes, ma'am. I see her quite well, thank you. I will give you thirty dollars for her and not a penny more. She is a fine specimen, fine indeed."

Before I could say boo, the transaction was done, and the man was ushering me out of the house without any of my belongings or letting me say goodbye to my siblings. I turned for one last look at my home just as my mother tucked the money in her brazier with a smile on her face. I was too shocked to do much of anything but follow the man out.

I had been raised to obey, and if not, I would take a beating, but honestly, was I only worth thirty dollars to my mother? What about my brother and sister? Who was going to watch them now? I knew my mother wasn't going to take no heed of them. Were they going to be sold next? So many thoughts flew through my head as I watched the man's feet in front of me. With my head bowed, I heard the front gate squeak one last time as it closed, and we were headed down the lane. My mother had given me nothing and no time to pack. The life I knew was gone; the only place left to go was forward.

Chapter Four
She will do

"Are you cold?" He asked. His voice was vibrant; it did not match the outside of him at all. It was nothing like the gravelly voice I had heard him use in the house. It was almost as if there were two different people that had spoken. I glanced up at him through my stringy hair to make sure it was the same man who had been in my house a few moments ago. It was.

"No sir, I'm fine. Thank you." I fought hard to hold back the tears. I think he might have been able to hear my voice break, but I didn't care. I wasn't sure why I was crying, except I didn't know what the future held for me. At least at home, there was a routine. I knew what to expect from day to day. I had no idea what this man would want from me. Why had he not let me grab anything? Was he going to kill me?

We walked for a bit more in silence. I think the quiet made him uncomfortable. I realized I craved the silence. After caring for small children day in and day out, silence was, as they say, golden. I finally had a moment for my own thoughts, to hear my own voice. It was shocking to realize that I would not hear the little voices of my siblings screeching and laughing again. I sighed in contentment at the idea of being able to speak at a normal volume and not have to yell. I almost smiled at the thought of the silence.

"I'm not going to touch you. I know that was not what your mother implied to you, but you are safe from that with me." I just looked up and nodded. In my experience, grownups rarely told the truth.

We walked for what seemed like forever. It was dark before we arrived at a small house surrounded by, well, nothing. There was no farm to work or store to mind. It was just nothingness. A dark nothingness that chilled me to my bones. As we approached, the door swung open, and a voice called out, "you're late."

The man just grunted and walked into the house. A younger man, a few years older than me or so, stood tapping his foot impatiently for me to pass before he closed the door behind us. I scooted through the door, doing my best not to touch the man standing there while still following the grey man. The warmth of the room hit me, and I looked up to examine my surroundings. The house was big, bigger than my old house had been. And much better kept, which didn't speak highly of me since I was the keeper of the last house. A wonderful smell seemed to engulf me as soon as I stepped in. The younger man stood with his arms crossed, looking me up and down.

"Is this her? Will she do?"

"Yes, yes. She will be fine. Why don't you get her some food and see if you can't find a better-fitting dress or something for her to wear." I looked down and realized the gap in my buttons had left my chest area exposed. I had underclothes on today, so I had not noticed a draft, and honestly, I was so used to this I'm not sure I would have. I tugged the two sides of the shirt together, hoping to close off the gap a bit, but when I let go, it just opened again. I crossed my arms over my chest and put my head down lower, wishing these two men would not notice me.

The younger man grunted in almost the same fashion as the older man had just a few moments before, turning toward a large metal pot that hung over the open fire in the huge fireplace. He scooped up a bit of whatever was in the pot, sloshed it into a bowl, and then turned back toward me. He gestured with his head that I should sit at the table, then he placed the bowl down in front of a chair and turned to grab a spoon and a napkin. We didn't use napkins in our house. They were for fancy homes. We just wiped our hands on our clothes and wiped our mouths with our hands.

I stood hesitating momentarily, unsure of what was truly expected of me. There was no way that they were going to feed me before making me do any chores. I thought about this and about trying to bolt out the door, then my stomach growled, and I gave in to the idea of a hot supper. As I sat, the young man placed a glass of what I assumed was milk in front of me and a large piece of crusty bread. I looked up and nodded my thanks to him. Never meeting his eyes, I dug into the food.

It wasn't eggs! I was so excited that I wasn't eating eggs I didn't even ask what it was. I just gobbled it down in a very unladylike manner while gulping down the big glass of fresh milk. The young man snorted and tossed a dish towel on the table so I could wipe my face since I had scrunched up my napkin, leaving it almost unusable. I had never tasted anything so good! If this was going to be my last meal, at least it was a good one. If it wasn't my last, well, then I'd need to find out what was in it so I could make it again someday.

"You can sleep in there," He pointed at a loft above the main room. "I'll have to search in the morning for better-suiting clothes. Do you have anything else to wear?"

Everything the younger man said was short and abrupt. He looked me square in the face each time he spoke but never seemed to meet my eyes. This was fine with me. I knew better than to meet a man's eyes that brought unwanted attention or a beating. Neither of which I cared for this evening.

I shook my head but kept my head down. "Okay, hang on. Here." He handed me a large man's shirt. "You can sleep in this. Toss the dress down, and I will clean it. I'll have fresh clothes for you in the morning." I nodded slightly as an acknowledgment but never spoke. I was afraid to break whatever spell was going on. Fresh clothes to wear, a scrumptious, hot meal, and now a bed to myself! If this wasn't heaven and I wasn't cold and dead somewhere, I did not want to find out. I was going to take as much of this as I could!

"There is a pitcher with water and a bowl up there. A towel to wash with. I'm sorry it isn't warm. I wasn't sure when you would be getting in, so I just prepared as best I could. You can dump the dirty water out the window up there when you are done, don't worry about hitting anything. There's nothing out there, and we will be in for the night."

He took my bowl from the table and turned away, effectively dismissing me. I climbed the ladder to the loft and washed, then changed into the oversized shirt, tossing my dress down as I had been instructed. I opened the window and poured the dirty water, then neatly placed the bowl next to the pitcher. I had left enough water in the pitcher in case I got thirsty throughout the night. I finally climbed into the bed. It was soft and warm and empty. No little bodies to share it with, no feet stuck in my ribcage, or tiny hands laying on my face. I slept better that night than I had in my whole life. I am sure I smiled all night in my sleep.

Chapter Five
The Vessel

In the morning, a new dress was draped on the chair next to the mattress. I must have slept through the younger man climbing up and placing it there. I was delighted to put it on. It fit perfectly. I did a little spin and took a deep breath to see if I would pop the buttons, and I didn't! I was giddy with joy at having something that fits so well, and it was new! I don't know if I had ever had a new dress before. In fact, I was positive that I had never had a new dress before! I almost didn't want to go down the ladder. I wanted to spend the day feeling pretty in my new dress. I wanted to appreciate that clothing could fit so well and not make me feel as if my chest were going to pop out at any second or that I was only worth scraps from everyone else's clothes. I wanted to relish the quiet, as well as the lack of responsibility.

But I knew I had to go down; they might have other things for me that I needed to do to pay for my accommodations.

I slowly descended the ladder into the main room. Both men were up already, though I had not slept late as the sun was barely over the horizon. These two seemed to have been up way before the sun even thought of rising. It was also nice not to be the first one up, the one that had to get the fire going and the food made for everyone. Even if they did have chores for me, I kept thinking I could get used to this kind of life.

The older man was sitting at the table reading a book and writing something down as he hummed to himself. The younger man was working in the kitchen again. He came out with a plate of eggs and toast for me and a strong cup of coffee. I nodded my thanks and sat down to eat. These eggs tasted a million times better than any I had ever made. They had salt in them and pepper. There was some kind of green herb in them as well that I could not identify. And I did not have to cook them! Whatever it was that made them taste so good, it was divine!

The old man started talking to me, never looking up from his book, so it took me a moment to even realize he was addressing me. "Child, I have a job for you today. I have a plot out back that needs to be turned into a garden. Do you think that's something you could do?"

I looked at him for a split second longer than I should have before ducking my head down, "yes, sir, that's something I can do."

"Good, good. I will have Randolph show you where the tools are. It's a fine day to work outside!"

That was the end of any of the conversation. He went back to his book and his humming. I finished my breakfast and got up from the table, unsure of what to do with my dirty plate and utensils. Randolph grunted that I should leave them on the table, then motioned for me to follow him out back to show me where they wanted the garden and where the tools were. He grunted some more at me. The only word spoken was "here." He then went back inside, leaving me to make the garden plot.

The day was getting hot as I was finishing up with the turning of the soil. I decided to make the plot so that it would face the sun for the cooler part of the day. It got so hot here that most things just burned in the summer. From where they wanted me to turn the soil, I knew they had no clue how to garden. I was okay with doing this task for them if they would clothe me and do the cooking; gardening was fun when it wasn't the only thing to eat. I walked around the outside of the house to find some water when I overheard them talking out on the front porch.

"Do you think she will be a good vessel? She seems a bit off."

"She should be perfect, Randolph. She has just enough fear and submissiveness to be the perfect host. Trust me, I have watched her for months making sure we are choosing the exact vessel we need."

I slid behind the side of the house, where they wouldn't see me. Submissive, eh? Well, they might be in for a surprise if they thought I was going to lay still and let anything happen. If living in the squalor of my mama's house had taught me anything, it was how to survive. I knew how to keep my eyes down and my ears open. I knew that strength wasn't always who could yell the loudest but who could stand the longest. I was done with anyone telling me what to do, yes, I had made their garden, but if they thought that I would be a slave or worse, a whore, they had another thing coming. I knew I was just biding my time doing their chores, waiting for my chance to break free.

Chapter Six
The Trade

Evening came quick, as it does toward the end of the summer season when the air starts to get cool and the sun sets earlier. Randolph cooked stew and made sure I had more than enough, along with some fresh brown bread. No words were spoken again except by the older man. He made benign chatter about the weather and the plot I had created for a garden. He smiled at me a lot. I did my best to look back at him blank-faced.

"We are having a bit of a celebration tonight. The three of us. We are so grateful to have you join us. We are grateful to have food on our table, a roof over our head, and now a new garden to bring in the end of the summer."

I nodded. The old man asked me to help move the table aside so the area in front of the fireplace would be clear. As the table was moved, a circle was revealed to be drawn on the floor or painted, I couldn't tell really, but it did not come up when I scraped my shoe over it.

"It's rather dark in here, don't you think? Why don't you help me light a few of these candles and place them around the room? That's right. Around the circle will be fine. Good girl." The old man directed me where to place the candles, they were the basic beeswax kind, but someone had colored them, so they looked like a dirty soot color, all dark grey with swirls of black. I had never seen anything like this, but I thought some people were just odd. As long as no one kicked one and burned the place down, I didn't really care where they wanted the candles.

The fireplace was bright enough to light the whole room without any help, with a roaring fire and a large pot hanging over the open flame, the room was rather warm. Something bubbling in the big pot smelled awful, nothing like the wonderful stew we had eaten for dinner. I wondered where that had gone and when it was replaced with whatever was making that awful stench. I realized I really should pay more attention to my surroundings if I were to stay safe. This thought alone made me take note of everything around the room, the two men, the circle, the fire, and the stench. They all combined to make me uneasy.

The older man sat a chair in the circle and smiled at me. I did my best not to look up at him as he came over and took me by the shoulder, and steered me into the chair. I kept my eyes down to the ground, never letting them know I had heard what they said earlier in the day. Never once letting them think that I could be more, more than they bargained for and more than they thought.

"This is for you." Motioning to the whole room, "You are the reason we will have a garden and fresh vegetables this year. Thank you." He folded his hands in front of him like in prayer and bowed to me, then handed me a yellow handkerchief and stepped out of the circle. I looked up and noticed the candles that had been lit all around the circle were giving off a yellow smoke. Both men looked at me and smiled, then began to chant in a language I did not understand.

"Tasa Fubin Maymon Oncar, Tasa Fubin Maymon Oncar, Tasa Fubin Maymon Oncar"

It felt as if the chanting went on for hours, but it must have just been a few moments before I began to feel the air shift around me. It got thick and began to weigh down my shoulders. There was a slight smell of rotten eggs in the air; it was getting harder to see the men, as if they were fading away from me. It was like the air was full of heat. Everything was all wavy and distorted like the fields look in the dead of summer.

I sat still in my chair, wondering what was going to happen to me, but not willing or able to stand and move away. I was curious now. This was not what I thought this night would bring. I thought the two men had more nefarious ideas than to sit me in a circle surrounded by parlor tricks. I smirked at the idea of just sitting here while they chanted all night. I wondered if I would be able to sleep in this chair or if I should get down and curl up on the floor.

A yellow smoke began to seep all around me, filling the space inside the circle. Just when I could not see beyond my own nose, I felt a presence. There wasn't a solid shape that I could see, just the feeling I was not alone. Fingers brushed my hair. I was too scared to move at this point. The drumming of my heart in my chest gave away my fear. I felt a finger brush the hair out of my face. I felt hands running up and down the sides of my body as if assessing a side of beef. I still did not look up or acknowledge that there was anything with me.

"Fear Me!" echoed through my mind. I took a breath and looked up with just my eyes, keeping my head down, my hair spilling over my face.

"No." that one word whispered into the night.

I lifted my head and stood. I stood as tall as I could, straightening my shoulders and surrounding myself with the arrogance that my mother carried with her. I had learned this from watching her. I knew this was a way of being powerful in my own right.

"No, I will not fear you. I invite you. Please allow me to be your vessel." I put my hand on my hip and cocked it. I stood before this thing, knowing this was my way out. Feeling the power my mother must have felt when she posed in this same way, knowing all eyes were on me.

I felt the shock of the being. It wanted me to fear it. It wanted to control me, to devour me. I sneered, knowing the men outside the circle couldn't hear me. Knowing this was just between the entity and me. I felt it waver as the chanting got louder.

"Come on, you need a vessel for life, and I need a life. Fair trade. I give myself freely."

I felt it consider the offer. I felt the heaviness of its acceptance. Then the world went black.

Chapter Seven
We Meet

I came into myself, standing inside the circle, watching the two men fight. There was blood and fists flying as they tried to beat the life out of each other.

I could feel my face smiling. Lifting my hand in front of my eyes, I was aware I was looking at things as if they weren't happening to me but more as if I was watching a show. I looked at my hand, realizing my stance had changed. Instead of slouching to hide my figure, I was standing up straight and with a hip thrown out in the same seductive pose my mother used, but I was doing it well! So well that my mother might have been jealous of me! I felt sexy, powerful, and wonderful. This felt good, whatever this was.

They are fighting because of us. A voice in my head cackled.

Why? What did we do? I asked back.

We just are. This is what we do. Only with you, we are more. You are a vessel for the ages. With this body and myself, we will rule the world.

I was confused for a moment, but then pride started to overtake my confusion. Pride at what I had done, pride in my looks, pride in my power.

Yeasssssss. That's why we will make a great team.

Randolph stood over the old man, bloody from the beating given and taken. His breathing was ragged, his right arm hung at an odd angle.

I gave an exaggerated sigh and started to fan myself as if it was very hot in the house.

"Wow, Randolph, I didn't know you were so strong. I would love to feel those muscles, but I'm stuck in this circle." I felt my eyes go big as if I was about to cry, and my lips felt as though they were pouting. I put all the sadness I could conjure up into my eyes and looked at him as if he were the sole person left on the earth. I felt one single tear roll down my cheek. With a thought, I pushed all this sadness and loneliness out into the air and directed it towards him. I knew when it hit him he felt how much I wanted him, how lost I was without him.

He almost tripped over the body of his one-time friend, trying to get to the circle. He used his foot first to try to erase the line, but it had been painted onto the floor. He started to panic and run around the room while we stood there and smiled sadly at him. He grabbed a knife and tried chipping away at the circle. He gave up the knife as all the blood on his hands made the knife slip too much, and ran outside. He came back in with some paint thinner and a rag. He began to wipe away at the circle. He scrubbed and scrubbed down on his hands and knees until there was a clear spot in the circle, just large enough for us to step through.

We walked past him and smiled down as he looked up from his prone position.

"Thank you so much, sir. I am forever grateful. What could I possibly do to repay you?"

We blinked our eyes ever so slowly and threw him a come-hither smile. He scrambled to his feet, eyes wide like a child looking at Santa Clause.

"Ma'am, if I could have a night with you, my world would be complete."

Of course, it would, we thought, *pride and lust. Our two favorite things. Pride to believe he was worthy of us, desire just for us. Now we just needed a little anger mixed in for it to be a complete meal.*

We looked down at ourselves. We were still in the same dress he had brought to us. Our hair was still greasy, and our body still dirty. The outside seemed the same on the surface, but there was a pull. We knew we could have whatever we wanted; of course, everyone wanted us. Why wouldn't they? We were beautiful, intelligent, funny, and sexy. We would be unstoppable if we could just get cleaned up a little.

We walked over to him and gently brushed his face with our fingertips, ensuring our breasts touched his arm ever so slightly.

"Of course, anything for you. First, though, I would like to bathe. I am feeling so dirty from the day."

"Yes, ma'am."

"Oh, and love, you know my name." We smiled and giggled as we said this. "You called me, remember? Maymon, but just because it's you, you can call me May."

He blinked. We thought we might have made a mistake reminding him that he summoned us from the underworld. We threw lust and want into our eyes; our stance became more seductive. He blushed.

"Yes, ma'am, I mean May." He stuttered as he looked down at the floor and shuffled his feet like a child caught in the act of doing something wrong. We could see by the fit of his pants that he was very happy we were there. Nothing childish about that. We smiled at him again.

"Umm, I'll go fetch the water for the tub. It's in the back room over there. I hooked it up so that there could be hot water if we kept a fire burning outside. You can take a nice hot bath if you'd like."

"Oh, you are a smart man, aren't you. Yes, that would be lovely. I will wait for the water to be brought and heated. Thank you for doing this."

He blushed again and hurried out.

Chapter Eight
Life Begins

The water was warm on our skin. The boy had done an excellent job of gathering enough water and keeping it warm so that we could immerse our whole body under warm water. The soap was something other than what we would typically have chosen, though. Of course, anything was better than the dirty skin and hair we started with.

For the most part, our mind was equally divided now. May was more extroverted and more in control than the girl, but she was still here. She kept us in check a little, though she always wanted to be the type of woman May was allowing her to be, so that hesitation was not nearly as strong as it could have been. She was excited to explore all the things she never thought she would get to.

"May, I brought some towels for you. Can I get you anything else? Food, water?" Randolph stood in the doorway, still covered in the dried blood of his friend, eagerly wringing his hands as if in anticipation of what was to come.

We stood up and let the water drip down our body. We put our hand out so the boy knew to help us out of the tub. He scurried over and lifted us, dripping out of the tub, his hands nearly encircling our waist as he lifted. We let out a deep chuckle and let his hands linger just a little longer on our body before we gently took the towel from him.

"Thank you, hon. Now, what is it we could do for you?"

He ran his hand over our shoulder and down the outside of the towel, stopping to cup our behind.

"I want you." He tried to look us in the eyes but quickly turned his head.

He stepped closer and tried to take us in his arms. The dried blood smeared on our clean body. The towel dropped as he stepped closer.

"Now, love, why would we want to waste ourselves on someone such as you. What do you have to offer us?" We pushed him off us with a sneer. Then ran our hands up and down our body. It was a nice body, curvy and young. The skin was so tight not one single wrinkle was visible. As our hand moved, we appreciated the youth. We were more than we ever thought possible when we heard the call from these two losers. This was going to be a great vessel. We hoped to keep it fresh. We wanted this one for a long time to come.

"I..I...I freed you! You owe me!" He stood before us, getting angrier and angrier as we teased him with our hands on ourselves. His face turned red, then a slight shade of blue. The bulge in his pants must have been uncomfortable. The idea of his discomfort made us work harder to increase it. His anger and lust were tasty, but the discomfort was like the cherry on top of our meal. So refreshing!

"Yes, yes, you did." We took a step toward him, just out of reach. "You freed us; you gave us this wonderful body. Do you know who we are?

"Maymon! You are Maymon, demon king of the south, lieutenant to Satan himself, and you must answer to me!"

Our laughter echoed through the room. "I am King. I answer to no one." We sneer at the boy.

"King of the demons of the south, demon of pride, lust, and anger. Yes, I know. I called you, made you mine, and put you in the body of a woman. Women are below men in the hierarchy of heaven and hell; thus, you answer to me!" The boy's face was going from red to purple in his rage and fear. We just laughed.

"King, queen, it's all the same to me. I am not man nor woman, I am Maymon. Now let me feel that sweet rage."

We closed our eyes, opened ourselves up, and drank in the boy's rage. It was sweetly sour, much like a lemon. It filled us. Made our body fill out more in places it needed. Our hair became more lustrous, our eyes twinkled more, and our lips plumped up just enough. When we were finally full, we opened our eyes to see the boy standing in front of us, depleted. His head hanging down, his arms drooped to his side, there was little left of the feisty young man who had tried to order us around.

"That's a good boy. Now, why don't you go to town and fetch us a new dress. Something modern, expensive, and green." We patted him on the head as if he were a puppy.

He looked up, his eyes were drawn, and his color was slightly grey. Ah yes, we had fed well. Maybe one more meal from this one. But for now, we needed him to fetch and carry for us. We could not be seen in this old dress.

"And shoes, black. Go. Now. I expect you back before nightfall. Take the money the old man had hidden. You know where it is." And with that, he was gone. We didn't bother to put the dress back on. It smelled of sulfur and really was not worthy of us anymore. We stayed in our nakedness, sure that not a soul would come around this way. We went and sat in the yard, letting the sun warm our body. The night seemed to have passed while we were becoming one. We drank from the well and ate leftover stew. The food made us wonder if we shouldn't keep the boy around. He was a fantastic cook! As the sun began to set, we saw him trudging back to us, sweaty and dirty. Remnants of blood still on his clothes. We should have made him wash and redress before he went. We would need to be more careful in the future.

The boy came back before nightfall as directed and was wildly successful at getting a dress for us, which we were actually a little surprised at. The nearest town was small and poor, we did not expect much, but the dress he returned with would do splendidly. It was not quite the green we wanted, but it was new and in style. An olive-green midi flapper dress with a v-neck and a bow at the collar. There was a thin belt that we adjusted to go over our hips so it would enhance our movement. The shoes were a flat black with a small heel. He even got us one of those hats that would cover most of our hair. All in all, we looked quite stylish.

"Thank you, you may go clean up the house now. Probably best if you buried the body before daylight. Don't want anyone wandering in and seeing that."

He nodded defeatedly. Maybe he would not supply another meal. Oh well. Tomorrow we would head to town to see what we could find.

Chapter Nine
Our Next Meal

The day dawned bright. The sky was a myriad of reds and oranges with clouds that looked like an artist had just run his brush quickly across the sky without a care as to how it would turn out. The fields around the small house were covered in shimmering dew, the fresh smell of the morning air was intoxicating. All things that would bring joy to anyone's heart, but we were too busy thinking of where to get our next meal. We looked past the beauty of the world and turned to look for the strife.

The boy was useless to us now. Sullen and shrunken into himself, he hid away in the farthest corner of the house. We didn't even get to eat his ego which had been on full display that first night. Ah well, at least he was useful to us for a while, but now it was time to go. We were sure we could find someone to feed off soon. We had a whole town of people to choose from. Feeding was important, for each feeding brought us more and more power. If we went too long between them, we lost a little of that hard-earned power. The types of feedings mattered as well; feeding off emotions allowed us to manipulate more emotions while feeding on the pride of others kept us beautiful and young. Both resources were needed to keep us moving toward our favorite type of feeding, lust.

Now lust, lust was our most enjoyable feeding. It allowed us to control. We could control the desire, yes, but most humans bowed to their lust, followed it, let it control them. This meant we gained more power if we could make them lust over us. For the most part, lust was an individual desire. The lust was brought on by us, our body, our attitude. We controlled the way we acted; thus, the lust of us was a tiny bit of control over that person. That meant feeding on lust would give us the power to control anyone we wanted. Well, to an extent, some, very few, but some were immune to this. For them, we made sure to find their other weakness. Then we fed off that. We could pretty much feed off any human. They all have some sort of weakness. But the main ones to make us grow were the big three: pride, greed, and lust.

We headed into town, not bothered by the long walk. It was cool and gave us time to adjust to our new body. We were most solidly we by this time. Our personalities were meshing with such precision as if she were made for me. We enjoyed the sensation of each other as we walked. With each step, we adjusted to the swing of the hips, the way the feet landed on the pebbles. Our knees and back had to be made to stay straight. The girl had always tried to stay as small as possible, so we needed to reteach the body how to strut and look confident. We looked around through new eyes. The sunlight felt so bright! The colors jumped at us. By the time we walked the distance to town, we were sure we would need sunglasses, but we had also adjusted to the movements of this body.

`The town, of course, was small. The depression, coupled with the dust bowl, had hit this area harder than most. Main street was mostly shuddered buildings. Dirt and dust blew down the empty road covering it partially. We had no idea where the boy had found this dress, but we don't ask many questions as long as we get what we want. We were just hoping perhaps we, too, could find the store and purchase another similarly styled dress.

We sashayed down the sidewalk, winking and finger-waving at anyone that stared too long. Jealous. We loved the jealous. So easy to feed on and so prevalent. They saw what they wanted to be, rich, comfortable, and confident. We inhaled and fed off of them. It felt so good! No lust just yet, but give it time. The right man, or woman, would cross our path soon.

We headed into the diner at the edge of town, it was just as dingy as the town, but the aroma of fresh coffee and breakfast seemed like heaven. We found a stool on the corner of the counter, propped ourselves on the high seat, crossed our legs, and leaned onto the counter as if we wanted to order.

The waitress that came over looked tired. Not old or ugly, just tired. We felt no jealousy from her. In fact, we felt nothing. She was already a shell of a person, not a meal. We dismissed her as any use to us.

"What can I getcha, hon?" Her tired voice reminding us that we needed to try to fit in.

"May I have the flapjacks and a glass of water? And where might I find an office to look for a job?"

"You ain't from around here. There ain't no jobs, hon. Might as well keep moving on. Probably your best bet is to head down to Tulsa. They ain't been hit as hard as most us." She handed us the water she had poured from a pitcher kept behind the counter and headed back to her dreary world.

"I might be looking for some help." The voice came from behind us. We smiled and turned in our seat. Making sure that our legs came uncrossed just enough so he could let his imagination go.

With his eyes glued to our legs, we knew we had found our next meal.

Chapter Ten
Movin' on Up

In the next few weeks, we ate our fill. His lust kept us full and beautiful. In fact, it was enough to carry us through for months after. He wanted us each and every day. He would swat our bottom, drop papers and pencils, and ask us to bend over to get them. We made sure our dresses were just short enough to give him a peek. He knew he could have us; he was the mayor, after all. Who else would be worthy of us in this podunk town?

With all the lust to feed us, it was like an extra special dessert to feed on his pride too. His pride was the sweetest meal we had in eons. We sipped it like a fine wine, drawing it out, making it last. With each passing day, we got more powerful. This man who was so full of himself, with pride, power, and lust, shrank in little by little as fed.

Most of the women and some of the men in the town were full of jealousy. It was so thick that we didn't even have to try. We swam in it. This we also sipped. Our hair got healthier, our figure got curvier, our lips got poutier, each and every day, we became more. More of everything. It was a delicious feast. Until we were fully satiated.

We drained him financially and emotionally. We left a shell of a man where once stood a prideful, lust-filled mayor. We thanked him the day we left. We made sure he understood that he had done this to himself and that he had made us stronger, more able to feed on others. We patted him on the behind and told him to take himself back to his wife, then we carried our luggage out to the taxi and turned east.

We took ourselves on to Tulsa, just as the waitress on that first day in town had suggested. There we found more food than we had seen in years. Men and women out to explore themselves. We loved to play the guinea pig. We would let them believe we had never done anything like that before. We would bat our eyelashes and pout our lips, stand with our eyes averted, or stare straight into their eyes. We would say things such as, 'No, we had never had that type of drink. No, we had never laid hands on a woman or had a man lay hands on us.' Everyone believed us, and we ate our fill.

Our power grew and grew. There was not a time or a place where we did not feed. Even when we attended a local church, the feeding was plentiful. It got to be so much that we could go years without feeding, though we never did. We loved the feeling of power of those who thought so highly of themselves. We loved our youth. We loved how easily we could move from place to place and never get questioned. With the girl's looks and youth and my brain, we lived the best life, though, without each other, neither of us would have enjoyed so much freedom. We knew we were depended on one another, and we relished our duality.

Chapter Eleven
The Freedom

"We spent the decades traveling the country, feeding on those we could, destroying those we wanted to and, honestly, having the time of our lives.

Through the thirties and the beginning of the forties, the depression still raged in the majority of the country. If there was one thing we did not want to do, it was spend more time in a place where poverty and depression were more prevalent than pride and lust. So we spent most of our time in Hollywood. The glamour! We ensured we never got a role higher than a chorus girl in any movie. When the directors or producers would woo us, tell us we could be so much more, that we could be a star, we would take all of that in, their lust was delicious, and each one gave us enough to feed off of for months if not years, but of course, we always went back for more.

We made sure we changed our name and appearance as much as possible between directors. Each director thought we were a new, fresh face. It never occurred to them to check any other reels. Our names had changed, but really, in a time when plastic surgery was not too common, our features remained very much the same. The all-powerful pride kept each and every one of these men from telling the story of how some chorus girl had gotten one over on them. We did our best not to drain them, a sip here and a sip there was all we needed. We did, however, drain as much financially as we could. This, too, would sustain us for years to come and allow us to live the lifestyle we were entitled to.

Oh, and World War Two! What an amazing time that was! Here I thought this country would sit it out and I would miss all the fun, but then Japan decides to attack. I know there must have been someone like me running the show over there. No human in their right mind would attack the most powerful country in the world, especially since they were doing their best to stay out of the conflict. We all know, of course, that Hitler was a demon. I don't mean like just a bad guy. A similar circumstance was going on there as with the girl and I. Oh, you didn't know that? Well, how else could a lowly, crazy housepainter become one of the most powerful men in the world? I must say, I am a bit jealous of that lucky demon. All that destruction to feed off of. All that pride too, that lucky bastard must still be full from all of that. Yes, yes, he did die. Well, the body died. With all the strength that demon received, I am pretty sure he is still out in the world today. It would take more than just the mere death of its vessel to put it back in the under. Besides, look at all the evil that is around today. I am positive that guy is just bouncing from evil to evil now, looking for his next Hitler.

What did we do during that time? Well, of course, we headed to Los Alamos, you know, where the H- bomb was being finished.

But why are we telling you all of this? These are stories for another time, another person. We love thinking of all the good times. It's sad to think of all that in the past now. I will say one last thing about it, the sixties were extraordinary! So much lust! Oh, I could just wax poetic about then, of course, love, it was nothing like now. I think the eighties will go down as the best feeding we have ever had!"

We smile down at the man. Standing over him, our hands on our naked hips.

"Why are you telling me this? I've been here for days. Just, please, let me go." Tears started to leak out of his eyes. He couldn't wipe them, not with his hands cuffed to the bed frame. He lay spread eagle on the big, sumptuous bed. He had decided to bring us here, to Vegas, away from the prying eyes of his wife and family.

Like so many before him, he thought we were his to do with as he pleased. It never once occurred to him that we were using him.

"But dear, you asked. Remember? You asked why we were doing this to you. This is why. So we can feed and get more powerful. We do try to do as we are asked, especially from one as delectable as you."

We sit gently on the bed next to him, he tries in vain to shift away from us. We run a well-manicured nail down the center of his chest. The eighties seem to be the era of the hairy chest. We aren't overly fond of it, but it is a source of pride for many men. So, we accept it because pride is food, after all.

For a man who is such a powerful business and political beast, he does whimper and squirm a lot. We get on our knees and straddle him. Then slowly crawl up his body. The squirming is delightful. When we get to his face, we place our hands on either side of it so he has to look us in the eyes.

We smile seductively, and even in so much pain and fear, we can feel how happy he is to have us there. We close our eyes and breathe in all that wonderful lust and pride that still linger about from habit of his always being the best in the room, we guess. Oh, what is this? Just a hint of rage. Our smile gets wider. How wonderful! It has been decades since anyone had the nerve to be angry with us. Fear, pain, loathing even we were used to, but rage! Rage is such a rare treat, almost as if it is the caviar of our meal. We close our eyes to savor the richness of it.

Chapter Twelve
New Beginnings

The clanging of the casino greets us as we sashay in. That last meal had been delectable, we left the "Do Not Disturb" sign on the door. We are not totally sure he was breathing when we left, but thems the breaks sometimes, as they say. We had made sure to empty his wallet of cash and take any of the casino chips he had left strewn about. We left the credit cards, to easily traced. Now we were ready to try our hand at the games. Luck felt as though it were with us tonight.

A tall man with a full head of hair and a matching mustache eyes us over his sunglasses. Yes, we were satiated, but a little more would be lovely. We could always use more, more power, more youth, more everything. And if he was going to throw himself at us, why not. We toss our hair back, straighten our pencil skirt, and strut to where he is playing blackjack.

"Hi beautiful, what's your name?" His hand is already working its way up our thigh.

"May, my friends all call me May." We smile down at the man, letting him see in our eyes that we, too, are interested.

"Well, May, I think you and I might be great friends." His teeth gleam as he smiles up at us, his hand tickling our thigh.

"I think you might be right, sir." We continue to smile down, feeling lust and pride rolling off of him. How could we resist?

"Where are you from, sir." We sit on his knee and twirl our fingers in his hair.

"Oklahoma, ma'am, Cimarron, Oklahoma. And my name is Terrell. But you can call me Cowboy."

"Wow, Oklahoma, you say? I would just die to see it there. I hear the panhandle area is full of surprises."

We wink and stand up, grabbing his hand as we rise. "Why don't you show me all the things an Oklahoma man can do, and maybe I'll let you take me back there, Cowboy."

He throws his cards down and stands up, straightens his jeans with his one free hand, then wraps his arm around us. "I'd really love to take you back that way. Bet no one there has seen something as pretty as you before."

"Oh, I bet they have, at least a time or two."

Authors Note

Cimarron County Oklahoma is the westernmost county in Oklahoma. Throughout most of history Cimarron has had the smallest population in Oklahoma. Cimarron is known to have the lowest precipitation rate yet the highest snowfall rate.

In the past the area had been known as no mans land and was the place where many outlaws went seeking refuge.

During the depression and the dust bowl Cimarron County was one of the most effected areas in the country, with drought, tornadoes, blizzards, floods and dirt storms the people of the area had to do whatever they could to survive, this included selling

their children.

The characters in this book are fiction, but the hard times are based on real events.

Coming Soon

Dog Days

Chapter 1

The Poor Beast

"Fucking cows!" Jo muttered under her breath as she tore the last of the branches off the heifer so she could get back to the barn. She had noticed one heifer missing from the herd as they came in to get food. She was pretty sure this one was bred, so Jo wanted to make sure she hadn't given birth somewhere. The rain had started earlier in the day, but with all the other ranch chores, Jo hadn't thought too much about the wet weather until the thunder started rolling in. The rain was coming down in literal sheets as she tugged the last branch away. The cow took off, spraying Jo with what she hoped was just mud in its effort to get back to the herd. Jo quickly mounted her mare, a good old girl who had stood patiently as the rain pelted her.

"c'mon girl, let's make sure she can find her way back. We don't have to go searching again." She used the reins to turn the horse around, even though the mare was an old hack at this and moved with just the slightest shift in Jo's body, she wanted to hurry home to her warm shower and cozy bed.

The rain poured off the edges of her old Stetson; she wore her dad's old cowboy raincoat with its split sides, so her legs stayed relatively dry as she rode home. With rain such as this, though, no amount of rain gear could keep her totally dry.

Thunder rolled in the background; the flash of lightning lit the sky as bright as noon. In the corner of her eye, she saw a small furry thing lying in the mud. She tried to ignore it and urged the mare forward, trying to keep the heifer in her sight. Then, in that one moment of quiet before the next crash of thunder rolled over the prairie, she heard a small whimper.

Jo sighed, damned her soft heart, and turned to see what poor beast was drowning in the rain in mud out in her cattle fields.

She pulled the mare up short and hopped down; no need to step on the poor beast because it was dark, and she couldn't see quite clearly. She reached in her saddle bags, grateful her father had always told her to keep them "packed up for emergencies, no tellin' what you might need out in the dark and the rain."

Jo smiled at the memory; her dad was always one to be prepared. Or so she had thought.

As she reached the animal, she dropped to her knees and saw it was a small dog. A terrier-type from what she could tell. No color was discernible with all the rain and mud, but it was clear that he was terribly hurt.

"C'mon, boy, this isn't going to feel good, but at least if you die, you won't die alone." She scooped him up, surprised at how small his frame was. He must have been out for a while; he was so bony she knew the ride home wasn't going to be comfortable for her either. She threw him over the mares back in front of the saddle and swung up herself. She opened her raincoat and gently tucked him inside, then urged the mare forward toward the warmth of the house.

She carried the dog into the house, gently laying him on the old washing machine while she slipped off her boots and hung up her coat and hat to dry. The rest of her clothes would need to be changed soon, and a hot shower was in her future, but right now, this little guy needed her attention.

She found a towel still in the dryer, wrapped the mud-covered pup back up, and carried him to the fire. The fireplace was enormous! Big enough to heat most of the house at one time. Jo loved sleeping on the couch in front of the fire, so she rarely turned the heat on. With just her in the large home, there didn't seem to be a need to.

"Okay, buddy, as much of a mess as you are, I think tonight will just be about getting you warm, and hopefully, you'll make it through to morning." The brown eyes watched her as she laid down pillows and blankets, then placed him gently on top, still wrapped in the towel.

Being a working rancher, Jo had a good idea of what to do to help the little guy feel better. She quickly changed her clothes into warm sweats, then grabbed some goat milk out of the freezer. Goat milk was best for wayward baby animals. She heated it up as fast as she dared and grabbed a large syringe, the kind with the plastic, not the needle, and stepped back into the living room.

The room was full of shadows as the flames licked the top of the fireplace. Jo was surprised that the fire was going so well, but didn't question too much. "At least something's going right tonight."

She gently uncovered the little dog, who had dried while waiting for her. She rubbed it gently with the towel, knocking off as much mud as she could. The little dog flinched through most of this. Jo could see the claw marks all over the little guy. "Oh buddy, what did you get yourself into?"

She slowly fed him the whole bowl of goat's milk until his stomach was full and he had curled up on his makeshift bed. Gently, he started to snore. Jo stood and stretched, patted the dog, covered him back up with a blanket, and cleaned up the remnants of her first aid work. It was close to three in the morning, and her body ached from the day. The shower she was dreaming about would have to wait. She grabbed her big fluffy blanket that her great grandmother June had hand-sewn and was snoring right along with the dog in no time at all.

Don't miss out!

Visit the website below and you can sign up to receive emails whenever Terry Hooker publishes a new book. There's no charge and no obligation.

https://books2read.com/r/B-A-NSGX-IDKGC

BOOKS 2 READ

Connecting independent readers to independent writers.

Did you love *Ides of May*? Then you should read *Dog Days*[1] by Terry Hooker!

After the death of her father, Jo is determined to keep her family ranch. With a devious lawyer keeping her rightful inheritance from her while trying to forclose on the ranch so he can build a luxury resort and most of the townsfolk not believing a girl should run a ranch without a man around, Jo has to find a way to pay her bills and keep whats hers.

Help comes in the form of a small terrier left to die one stormy night in the middle of her cow fields. Little does Jo know that Buddy is not all he seems, with a bark that can shake the earth and the ability to bring tall dark strangers to her front porch, Buddy might be just what Jo needs to save her ranch.

Also by Terry Hooker

Devil's Land Stories
Ides of May
Dog Days

About the Author

About the Author: Terry Hooker is a bestselling author, freelance writer and editor, a Jersey girl from the shore turned Florida farm girl. She has a BA in anthropology, an AAS in Culinary Arts, and an MA in Library science. She has worked as a congressional archivist, historian, teacher, and professional chef and has presented her research on the history and iconography of southern cemeteries throughout the Southeast United States. She has edited several children's books, full length novels, dissertations, and academic papers; Terry, herself, has published scholarly papers, magazine articles, fictional stories, and books. She lives with her husband, two kids, and a plethora of critters.

You can follow her on Instagram: https://www.instagram.com/thooker_author or facebook: https://www.facebook.com/Terry-Hooker-Author